God Has a Plan
for Boys and for Girls

For Maya & Sophia

Written by
Monica Ashour, MTS, MHum

Illustrated by
Marilee Harrald-Pilz

*Love Tata
Patia*

Pauline
BOOKS & MEDIA
Boston

Library of Congress Cataloging-in-Publication Data

Ashour, Monica.
  God has a plan for boys and for girls / written by Monica Ashour, MTS,
M Hum ; illustrated by Marilee Harrald-Pilz.
       pages cm
  Summary: "This book attaches gender identity to being rather than doing
and reinforces common humanity and individual uniqueness"-- Provided by
publisher.
    ISBN 978-0-8198-3131-6 (soft cover) -- ISBN 0-8198-3131-X (soft cover)
  1. Sex role--Religious aspects--Christianity--Juvenile literature. 2. Gender
identity--Religious aspects--Christianity--Juvenile literature. I. Harrald-Pilz,
Marilee. II. Title.
  BT708.A785 2015
  233'.5--dc23
                                    2014046148

Cover and book design by Mary Joseph Peterson, FSP

Text copyright © 2015, Monica Ashour

Illustrations copyright © 2015, Daughters of St. Paul

"P" and PAULINE are registered trademarks of the Daughters of St. Paul.

Published by Pauline Books & Media, 50 Saint Pauls Avenue, Boston, MA
02130–3491

Printed in U.S.A.

GPBG VSAUSAPEOILL2-1710033 2393-7

www.pauline.org

1 2 3 4 5 6 7 8 9   19 18 17 16 15

Note to Parents, Guardians, and Teachers

As children grow and develop, they discover who they are. Receiving and forming one's identity as male or female is a critical part of that process. *God Has a Plan for Boys and for Girls* introduces and affirms the concepts of identity, human dignity, equality, and the purpose of gender.

- **This book helps prepare a child to realize that our human bodies "teach" us gender.** Everyone can say "I'm a boy," or "I'm a girl," with confidence and joy. Gender helps us to know ourselves. *I am male because I have a male body.* But the body also expresses who I am as a person to others. I have a female body *because I am female.*

- ***God Has a Plan for Boys and for Girls* helps kids to understand gender in a balanced way.** There are things all humans can do. Still, we can recognize that boys and men do things in a masculine way, and girls and women do things in a feminine way. Neither gender is *better than* the other; each is *different from* the other.

- **This book encourages children to acknowledge that God made some gifts for a *particular* gender.** Only a woman can be a mom, and only a man can be a priest. Because what we can see of a person reveals who that person is at a deeper level, we also see that reserving a gift for a particular gender is not something imposed by society or the Church. Instead, it has to do with the essence of the person as male or female.

In his Theology of the Body, Saint John Paul II underscores that masculinity and femininity are not interchangeable but complementary. God created women and men to balance each other with particular giftedness and approaches to the world. Male and female are part of God's plan and his purpose. As children journey toward adolescence, these principles are the foundation for discerning—and fulfilling—God's unique plan for them.

For more information and teaching ideas for this and other Theology of the Body principles, please visit www.pauline.org/tob4children.

Everybody is a person.

We all have human bodies and human souls,
human minds and human hearts.

We all hope for something—

that the sun will shine . . .

or that we catch a frog . . .

or that Lizzie can come along . . .

or that we don't have any homework today.

We're all afraid of something—

hairy monsters . . .

or bugs . . .

or the dark . . .

or falling down . . . or spelling tests.

We all like something best of all—airplanes . . .
or hamsters . . . or spinning in circles . . .

or making things . . . or the color blue.

Everybody is a person.

We all have human bodies
and human souls, human minds
and human hearts.

We all hope for something.
We're all afraid of something.
We all like something best of all.

God makes girls and boys alike in some ways.

Both of us can play sports and win the game.

We both like to read
books and ride bikes.
  Both of us want to
have friends and
learn math.

We both feel sad and alone sometimes. Both of us
can choose to give the last cookie to someone else.

11

When girls and boys
grow up they can both
work at hospitals or schools,
concert halls or TV stations, courts or banks,
churches or laboratories, or at home.

Boys and girls can do lots of the same things.
We just don't do things in the same way.

Everybody is a person.

We all have human bodies and human souls, human minds and human hearts.

We all hope for something. We're all afraid of something. We all like something best of all.

And we're all different. Each person— body, soul, mind, and heart—is unique.

There's only one you and only one me.

No one's fingerprint is the same as anyone else's.

Everybody is one-of-a-kind. There aren't any copies.

God has a special plan for each one of us.

And we're different. Each person—
body, soul, mind, and heart—is unique.
And God makes us boys or girls.

I'm a boy, inside and out.
My body is male.

When I grow up, I'll have
bigger muscles and a deeper
voice—maybe even a beard!
I will be a man.

I'm a girl, inside and out.
My body is female.
 When I grow up, I'll have
a soft, beautiful shape,
and a space for a baby
to grow inside!
 I will be a woman.

19

Everybody is a person.

We all have human bodies
and human souls, human minds
and human hearts.

We all hope for something.
We're all afraid of something.
We all like something best of all.

Still, we're different.

Girls can't be boys and boys
can't be girls.

But boys aren't better than girls, and girls aren't better than boys.

God makes girls special. It's good to be a girl.

God makes boys special, too. It's good to be a boy.

Boys and girls have something to give *and* receive.

Girls and boys have something to receive *and* give.

God has a plan for boys and for girls.

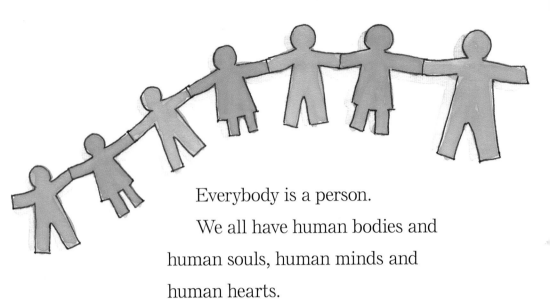

Everybody is a person.

We all have human bodies and human souls, human minds and human hearts.

We all hope for something. We're all afraid of something. We all like something best of all.

But even though we're different, women aren't better than men, and men aren't better than women.

God makes men special. It's good to be a man.

Only a man can be a husband, dad, or priest.

God makes women special, too. It's good to be a woman.

Only a woman can be a wife, mom, or a sister.

Men and women have something to give *and* receive.

Women and men have something to receive *and* give.

God has a plan for women and for men.

Everybody is a person.

We all have human bodies
and human souls, human minds
and human hearts.

We all hope for something.
We're all afraid of something.
We all like something best of all.

Still, we're different.

God has a plan for each
one of us.

God has a plan for each woman and each man.

God has a plan for each boy and each girl.

God has a plan for you and a plan for me.

Monica Ashour

National speaker, former teacher, and executive director of the Theology of the Body Evangelization Team (TOBET), Monica Ashour makes the depth and breadth of Saint John Paul II's revolutionary Theology of the Body (TOB) accessible. Building on her **TOB for Tots** series, Monica, who holds two master's degrees from the University of Dallas in the humanities and theological studies, goes one step deeper in **TOB for Kids**. These books make the mystery of the human person visible in the context of Catholic faith. Young and old alike will learn to see the BODY rightly: as a gift from God and a call to love. For more resources from TOBET, go to www.tobet.org.

Marilee Harrald-Pilz

Marilee Harrald-Pilz has been working as a freelance illustrator since 1979. After graduating from the University of Illinois with a BA in art education, she attended the Chicago Academy of Art, the American Academy of Art, and the School of the Art Institute of Chicago. A proud member of the Picture Book Artists Association, Marilee has primarily focused on the illustration of books, educational materials, magazines, and greetings cards for children. As a senior illustrator at Diamond Toy Company, she illustrated licensed characters, packaging, and display cards. Marilee has also worked as a designer of educational products at Cook Communications Ministries and Scripture Press Publications.

Marilee's work can be seen at:
www.MarileeHarrald-Pilz.com,
and www.storybookartsinc.com

Pauline
BOOKS & MEDIA

The Daughters of St. Paul operate book and media centers at the following addresses. Visit, call, or write the one nearest you today, or find us at www.pauline.org.

CALIFORNIA
3908 Sepulveda Blvd, Culver City, CA 90230 — 310-397-8676
935 Brewster Avenue, Redwood City, CA 94063 — 650-369-4230
5945 Balboa Avenue, San Diego, CA 92111 — 858-565-9181

FLORIDA
145 SW 107th Avenue, Miami, FL 33174 — 305-559-6715

HAWAII
1143 Bishop Street, Honolulu, HI 96813 — 808-521-2731

ILLINOIS
172 North Michigan Avenue, Chicago, IL 60601 — 312-346-4228

LOUISIANA
4403 Veterans Memorial Blvd, Metairie, LA 70006 — 504-887-7631

MASSACHUSETTS
885 Providence Hwy, Dedham, MA 02026 — 781-326-5385

MISSOURI
9804 Watson Road, St. Louis, MO 63126 — 314-965-3512

NEW YORK
64 West 38th Street, New York, NY 10018 — 212-754-1110

SOUTH CAROLINA
243 King Street, Charleston, SC 29401 — 843-577-0175

TEXAS
Currently no book center; for parish exhibits or outreach evangelization, contact: 210-569-0500 or SanAntonio@paulinemedia.com

VIRGINIA
1025 King Street, Alexandria, VA 22314 — 703-549-3806

CANADA
3022 Dufferin Street, Toronto, ON M6B 3T5 — 416-781-9131

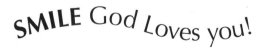

SMILE God Loves you!